Grandpa
Chatterji

Also by Jamila Gavin

I Want to be an Angel and Other Stories
Kamla and Kate
Kamla and Kate Again
Three Indian Princesses
Double Dare

for older readers

The Eye of the Horse
The Wheel of Surya
The Singing Bowls

JAMILA GAVIN

Grandpa
Chatterji

Illustrated by Mei-Yim Low

MAMMOTH

First published in Great Britain 1993
by Methuen Children's Books Ltd
Published 1994 by Mammoth
an imprint of Reed Consumer Books Ltd
Michelin House, 81 Fulham Road, London SW3 6RB
and Auckland, Melbourne, Singapore and Toronto

Reprinted 1994

Text copyright © 1993 Jamila Gavin
Illustrations copyright © 1993 Mei-Yim Low

The right of Jamila Gavin to be identified as author of this
work has been asserted by her in accordance with
the Copyright, Designs and Patents Act 1988

ISBN 0 7497 1716 5

A CIP catalogue record for this title
is available from the British Library

Printed and bound in Great Britain
by Cox & Wyman Ltd, Reading, Berks

Contents

1

'What are you doing, Grandpa?'

Neetu and her little brother Sanjay have two grandpas – Mum's dad and Dad's dad.

Mum's dad lives in India and they have never ever seen him. But Dad's dad lives in Leicester and they see him quite often.

Although they love and respect Dad's dad, as head of the family, Neetu and Sanjay are a little afraid of him. Whenever he comes to visit, they all have to be on their toes.

If Neetu wears jeans, Grandpa Leicester frowns at her and snorts, 'I don't like my granddaughter wearing jeans,' so she has to go and put on a dress. If Sanjay, who is a terrible chatterbox, sometimes interrupts, Grandfather glares at him sternly and says, 'I don't like little boys who interrupt,' and Sanjay has to bite his lip and try so hard not to speak.

When their mother got a job and went out to work, Grandfather was very disapproving. 'I don't like my daughter-in-law going out to work.' Mum just smiled politely, and went anyway, and Dad took his father aside to try to explain how with Mum going to work, they could afford a new car.

Perhaps the worst time is when Dad's dad comes to stay and they can't eat their favourite pizza and chips. Instead, they have to eat vegetable curry, runny spinach with eggs, and horrible stuff like that.

One day, Mum said excitedly, 'Children! Your grandpa is coming to stay! Isn't that wonderful!' But they didn't think it was wonderful at all. Neetu just groaned and said, 'Oh no! I'll have to wear nothing but dresses,' and Sanjay moaned, 'Oh no! We'll have to eat curried eggs.'

It was Dad who beamed at them and said, 'It's not my dad from Leicester who's coming to visit us, it's your Mum's dad from Calcutta. You've never met him! You can call him "Grandpa Chatterji".'

Neetu and Sanjay looked at each other doubtfully. How could they know whether a grandad from Calcutta was any different from a grandad from Leicester, even if he was called Grandpa Chatterji? They would just have to wait and see.

All that week Mum went round with a smile on her face, and even Dad seemed quite relaxed. Mum got the spare room ready, just as she always did for Dad's dad. But instead of worriedly scrubbing and cleaning and polishing and checking that there was not one speck of dust to be seen anywhere in the house, she actually hummed and sang and seemed to enjoy making everything look nice.

On the day of his arrival, Mum and Dad got up very early and drove off to the airport to meet Grandpa Chatterji. Neetu and Sanjay didn't go because there wouldn't be room in the car on the way back. Old Mrs Bennet from next door came in to look after them.

They waited and waited. Sanjay looked out of one window and Neetu looked out of the other. What would he be like? Would he wear a smart suit and shiny black shoes like Dad's dad? Would he smoke cigars and sit in the best easy chair and talk business with Dad in a big boomy voice? Would he have the best bed? Would he be served first at table? Would he always insist on using the bathroom first in the morning, even though he took the longest and made them late for school? And would he be critical and strict and insist on total obedience at all times?

They waited and waited. Suddenly, Sanjay shouted, 'They're here!' The little red Mini had pulled up outside the house.

'Oh dear,' cried Neetu, suddenly going all shy, 'I'm going to hide.'

They both hid behind the sofa. They heard the front door open. They heard Mum come in and say gently, 'Welcome to our home!' They heard Dad say, 'I'll take your luggage up to your room,' and they heard a thin, quiet, soft voice say, 'And where are my little grandchildren?'

Then there was silence. Crouched behind the sofa, Neetu and Sanjay hardly breathed. Then suddenly, although they didn't hear Grandpa Chatterji come into the room, they knew he was there because they saw a pair of bare, dark-brown, knobbly, long-toed, bony feet.

The feet came and stood right close by them. The feet emerged from beneath thin, white trousers, and as their eyes travelled all the way up, past a white tunic and brown waistcoat and past a red and blue woolly scarf round the neck, they found themselves looking into a round, shining, kind, wrinkly face, with deep-as-oceans large, brown eyes, and a mass of pure, white, fluffy hair which fell in a tangle over his brow.

'Ah!' exclaimed Grandpa Chatterji with a great, loving sigh, and he opened his arms to embrace them.

After they had all hugged each other, Mum said, 'Children, take Grandpa up to his room, he will want to bath and change after his long journey. I'll go and make a nice cup of tea.'

Sanjay began chattering as he clambered up the stairs, leading the way.

'Why aren't you wearing any shoes?' he asked.

'Because I took them off at the door, so as not to bring any dirt into the house. We always do that in India,' answered Grandpa Chatterji.

'Did you come with lots of suitcases, Grandpa?' Sanjay went on, 'and did you bring us lots of presents?'

'Ssh!' said Neetu, embarrassed. 'That's rude, Sanjay.'

'Just you wait and see,' replied Grandpa, who didn't mind at all.

When they went into the guest room, they couldn't see any suitcases at all.

'Where is your luggage?' asked Neetu.

'Oh, I only ever travel with my bedroll,' said Grandpa. 'My needs are very simple,' and he pointed to a roly-poly round khaki, canvas roll, all held together with leather straps, and covered in airline stickers and labels.

'Does that mean we don't have presents?' sighed Sanjay.

'Just you wait and see,' replied Grandpa again.

'You've got the best room in the house,' chattered Sanjay, bravely trying to ignore the mysterious roll which contained everything that Grandpa had brought.

'You've got the nicest sheets with duvet and curtains to match, you have the plumpiest pillows and the softest bed. It's the best bed in the house for bouncing on,' and Sanjay flung himself on to the bed, which Mum had made all smooth and neat, and he rumpled it all up.

'Sanjay!' cried Neetu with horror, dragging him off. 'Look what you've done,' and she tried to straighten it out.

'If you like this bed so much, you'd better sleep in it,' said Grandpa Chatterji. 'I prefer something harder.'

'Where will you sleep then, Grandpa?' asked Neetu looking worried.

'I'll sleep on the floor as I always do,' he replied. 'I am like a snail, my dear,' murmured Grandpa. 'All I need, wherever I go, is my bedroll. It carries all my belongings, and when I unroll it, it becomes my bed.'

The children looked in awe at the khaki, canvas roll. It suddenly seemed to be the most important thing in the world. 'Can we unroll it, Grandpa?' whispered Sanjay.

Grandpa bent over the roll and undid the old leather straps, then he slowly unrolled it alongside the bed. At first it seemed that all it contained was one sheet and one blanket. Sanjay was sure there were no presents; but then Grandpa wriggled his hand into the large pocket at one end of the roll and pulled out a tooth mug and toothbrush all wrapped in a towel, a hair brush and comb and his shaving things. Sanjay stared expectantly. Were there any presents?

Then Grandpa went to a pocket at the other end and wriggled his hand inside. He pulled out a woolly jumper, a woolly hat, some socks, underwear, hankies, a shirt, tunic and waistcoat, but still no presents.

At last, he folded back the sheet. Between the sheet and the blanket was a small, faded rug. He pulled back the rug to show lots of different packages.

'Presents!' breathed Sanjay, full of expectation.

'Why did you bring that old rug?' asked Neetu in a puzzled voice.

Grandpa Chatterji lifted it out as though it were the most precious thing in the world. 'I never go anywhere without this,' he murmured. 'It is my meditation rug. I sit on it to do all my thinking and praying.'

'Are those things presents?' asked Sanjay, pointing to the packages.

'Yes, yes, here you are,' laughed Grandpa. He handed Sanjay two long thin packages.

'Thank you, thank you!' yelled Sanjay, ripping them open. 'What are they?'

'One is a specially made, wooden wriggly snake, and the other is an Indian flute. Later I will teach you some tunes, but for now, you can just blow. It makes a lovely sound. Snakes love the sound of the flute. It makes them sway and puts them into a good mood.'

Sanjay flung his arms round his old grand-father. 'Thank you, thank you, Grandpa Chatterji!' and he rushed off to show his mum and dad.

Neetu waited patiently. Which package was for her? He bent over and handed her one of the larger ones. 'What a beauty you are, my dearest, little granddaughter! This is for you.'

When Neetu opened up her package, she found a beautiful pink and green and gold sari. It was a special small-sized sari for little girls. In India they have to wait until they are nearly grown-up before they can wear a sari, but all little girls love to have a sari they can dress up in, and this is what her grandfather had brought for her.

It made Neetu feel very solemn and proud. 'Oh thank you, Grandpa!' she declared in a grown-up voice, 'I'll go and ask Mum to help me put it on.'

Later, when Grandpa Chatterji had bathed and changed, Neetu, all dressed up in her sari, and Sanjay, with his snake and flute, went upstairs to find him. They knocked on his door.

'Come in!' he said in his soft, high voice.

They went in. Grandpa was sitting on the floor on his old rug. He was sitting very straight, his eyes staring in front and his arms stretched over his cross-legged knees.

'What are you doing, Grandpa?' asked Sanjay.

'I'm being a lotus flower floating quietly on a sea of milk.'

'Why are you being a lotus flower?' asked Neetu. She was looking like such a beautiful, grown-up lady in her new sari.

Grandpa looked at her and smiled with admiration. 'Come, children. Come and sit next to me. There's room on the rug.'

Neetu and Sanjay sat cross-legged one on each side of their grandfather. They stretched out their

21

arms over their knees and straightened their backs.

'We are being lotus flowers because we are trying to be as calm and peaceful and perfect as lotus flowers are,' explained Grandpa Chatterji, 'and if you close your eyes, you can imagine you are floating on a sea of milk before the creation of the world.'

The children closed their eyes and floated away.

Then Grandpa suddenly woke up with a shout and cried, 'I feel rested now! Come on! Where's that cup of tea your mother promised me? And while I'm drinking my tea, Sanjay can play the flute, and Neetu can dance! Will you?' he begged, his dark eyes glittering.

Neetu and Sanjay nodded with excitement. 'Oh, Grandpa Chatterji! We're so glad you came.'

2

'Ōm . . . Ōm . . . Ōm . . .'

When Neetu awoke the next morning, the first thing she thought was, 'Did Grandpa Chatterji really sleep on the floor?'

She sat up wide awake. It must be very early, because her room was still dark. Just a faint grey streak of light slipped between the curtains. Outside, the first blackbird had begun his dawn song.

She crept along to Grandpa Chatterji's room. His door was open. She peeped inside. At first she couldn't see anything. Then as her eyes adjusted, she saw that the spare bed, with its flowery duvet, was empty and hadn't been touched. On the floor, rolled out with a flat pillow and blanket was Grandpa Chatterji's bedroll; but there was no sign of Grandpa. Then she heard the sound. A slow, low repeating sound like the throbbing of a fridge, or the wind strumming the telephone wire. Or was it? Neetu listened carefully. Was it her own heart beating? No. Her heart was going boom, boom, boom, like a softly muffled drum. This sound was more like the waves beating against the shore; or a giant breathing . . . or . . ?

Ōm . . . Ōm . . . Ōm . . . The sound seemed to be everywhere; inside and outside. Was it Sanjay playing his flute? She tiptoed out of her bedroom and looked into her brother's room. He lay fast asleep, sprawled across his bed with his feet sticking out, and an arm flung over his best teddy. His wooden flute lay waiting patiently upon his pillow. Sanjay wasn't making the sound. Was it Dad snoring? She crept into her parents' bedroom. She saw their two humps side by side like bookends under the double duvet. She went closer and stood listening. But no, Mum and Dad were still so deeply asleep that you could hardly hear them breathing at all.

So she went downstairs, past the ticking clock in the hall, past the puff of the boiler as it fired the central heating, past the low throbbing of the fridge and up to the back door. Here, the sound· seemed louder. It was coming from the garden. Ōm . . . Ōm . . . Ōm . . . Was it the tree moaning in the wind?

She went outside. It wasn't a very big garden. Just a patch of lawn with two long flower beds running the length of the fence on each side. The best thing was the tree at the bottom. It wasn't the sort of tree anyone would plant. Its seed had been blown there by the wind long before Neetu was even born. It had grown quietly and secretly without anybody noticing. It had grown and grown till it was taller than their house. Its branches stretched out like lots of arms, and sometimes the wind blew around it making it creak and swish. It was where the blackbird sang his songs and where the sparrows caused kerfuffles among the clumps of ivy which clung to the trunk. But as Neetu stood outside the back door, she realised that it was a perfectly still morning, with not one breath of wind to even rustle the leaves. Ōm . . . Ōm . . . Ōm . . .

Then she saw him. Grandpa Chatterji was standing at the base of the tree. He wasn't wearing stripy pyjamas as Grandpa Leicester always did. He was bare-footed and was only wearing a thin white cloth wrapped round his waist and a white thread across his bare chest. He had spread out his precious rug, and he stood on one leg with his arms upstretched to the sky, as if he too were part of the tree.

Ōm . . . Ōm . . . Ōm . . . Neetu moved softly. She had nearly called out to her grandfather, but something told her not to. Silently, she walked across the grass and stood at his side. She looked up into his face. It was completely calm. His eyes were open, but he didn't look at her. He didn't even seem to know she was there. He breathed in a long, long breath which expanded his chest, and then he breathed out very very slowly. As he did, the deep, throbbing sound of Ōm soared through the air.

There was just room on the rug for Neetu. Without asking, she stood by his side. She tried to stand on one leg, but wobbled. She tried again, and managed to stand for a little longer. She raised her arms and looked up at the sky. Dawn was breaking through the grey branches, creating islands of pink clouds. Ōm . . . Ōm . . . She copied.

After a while, Grandpa Chatterji looked down at his granddaughter and smiled.

'What are we doing, Grandpa?' she whispered.

'We're praying to God and welcoming a new day. When you make a round shape with your lips and say "O" you are making the shape of the sun, the shape of the world and the shape of the universe. When you make the sound "Ōm" you are talking to the Creator of Everything.'

Then suddenly, Grandpa stopped being holy.

'I'm starving!' he cried. 'Let's make *pooris*!' He seemed to fly down the garden and into the kitchen. Neetu had to run to keep up.

'Where's the flour?' he asked.

Neetu found the flour.

'Where's the cooking oil?'

Neetu found the cooking oil.

'Where's the mixing bowl?'

Neetu found the mixing bowl.

'Where's the rolling pin?'

Neetu found the rolling pin.

29

Then Grandpa Chatterji put down his rug on the floor in a corner of the kitchen and began to mix the dough.

Sanjay came in playing his flute. He was still in his pyjamas and his eyes were sticky with sleep.

'Where have you been? I was looking everywhere for you,' he grumbled.

'Grandpa and I were saying hello to the sun,' explained Neetu. 'Look! We stood like this.'

Neetu stood on one leg with her arms up above her head. She breathed in deeply, and as she breathed out, she went 'Ōm . . .'

'That's easy!' scoffed Sanjay. 'I can do that!'

But when he tried, he wobbled all over the place.

'Come and help me with the *pooris*, you two!' interrupted Grandpa. 'Look! I've kneaded the dough. Now you take a handful and work it round into a ball. Then flatten it out on this wooden board and roll it into a circle with the rolling pin. I'll heat up the cooking oil.'

When the oil was smoking hot, one by one, Grandpa dropped the rolled out circles of dough into the sizzling pan.

'Look!' cried Neetu excitedly. 'Look how they puff up!'

'They're just like little footballs!' yelled Sanjay.

'They're round like Ōm,' said Neetu.

Soon they had a plate piled high with *pooris*.

Grandpa had boiled a kettle and made a big pot of tea. He said, 'Let's take your mother and father tea and *pooris* in bed!'

Neetu and Sanjay carried a plate each of *pooris* while Grandpa put five mugs of steaming hot tea on the tray. Then in procession, they climbed the stairs.

Mum and Dad sat up in amazement when they all trooped into the bedroom.

'*Garam Chai*!' announced Grandpa. 'Hot tea!'

'And *pooris* which we made!' boasted Sanjay!

'It's just like being back in India,' sighed Mum.

'These were always your mum's favourite when she was a little girl,' smiled Grandpa Chatterji.

'I think they're my favourite too,' cried Neetu with her mouth full.

Sanjay stood on one leg. He put his hands up above his head, and even though his mouth was full of *pooris*, he said, 'Ōm . . .'

3

Grandpa Rides in a Rocket

They knew the fair was coming to town, because one morning, bright posters were plastered all over the place on walls, in shops. They hung from hooks alongside the legs of lamb in the butcher's and the bunches of bananas in the greengrocers, or they were pinned on to notice boards in public buildings, in the library, in the town hall.

GRAND BANK HOLIDAY FAIR, the posters proclaimed. FUN FOR ALL THE FAMILY; AMUSEMENTS, STALLS, PONY RIDES, THRILLS AND SPILLS AND SPECIAL ATRRACTIONS.

'We must go to that,' said Dad. 'Keep a look out.'

Well, they didn't really need to keep a look out. You couldn't miss it. One day, all the roads through the town were clogged with battered cars

and vans, trailers and caravans, lorries and trucks. Clowns with silly faces mingled with the shoppers and thrust leaflets into their hands; a girl walked by on stilts, ten feet high, waving and smiling.

'I'd like to do that,' sighed Neetu.

When they went home and told Grandpa Chatterji about the fair, his eyes gleamed with pleasure. 'I love fairs,' he beamed. 'I love watching all the elephants and camels and horses and bullock carts, and all the women in their glittering skirts and saris, and all the men wearing their most colourful turbans. Oh good, oh good!' And he rubbed his hands together in anticipation.

'But, Grandpa,' exclaimed Sanjay in a puzzled voice, 'fairs here aren't like that.'

'You're thinking of an Indian fair,' laughed Mum. 'This will be quite different.'

'Oh!' said Grandpa, looking rather downcast. 'What will this fair be like?'

'It will have dodgem cars and merry-go-rounds and waltzers and a ghost train. It will have lots of stalls with games and competitions. I won a fluffy cat last year. I guessed the right number when I tossed in a coin,' Neetu told him.

'Grandpa, will you go on the rockets with me?'

begged Sanjay. 'Everyone else is too scared.'

'I'll go on anything,' boasted Grandpa, looking excited again.

'You'll remember your age, Pa, that's what you'll do,' said Mum firmly.

But Grandpa Chatterji couldn't remember his age. He was ageless. Sometimes he seemed as old and as wise as the universe, and other times, it was as though he had only just been born and had come into the world full of wonder. Now, he looked forward to the fair with all the excitement of a child. He rushed about saying, 'Come on, then. Let's go, let's go! What are we waiting for?'

'We'll go when its dark, Grandpa. It's much more fun,' they told him.

As soon as it was dark, the nearby playing fields were ablaze with light and loud music pulsated through the air. It was magic. No one could resist it. Everyone filled their pockets with money, and soon, all the roads leading to the fair were thronging with families. Mum, Dad, Grandpa, Neetu and Sanjay joined the crowds. Grandpa kept hopping up and down, his eyes wide as saucers. 'Look! Look!' He pointed at glittering machines which lit up the sky as bright as a city. He looked at the giant Rocket Ride, which rose up into the night like a space station,

37

its rockets orbiting and spinning like shooting stars. 'Let's see it all!' cried Grandpa Chatterji.

He was like a moth attracted by the fiery brightness. Not only were there garlands of fairy lights looped from stall to stall all bobbing about in the evening breeze, but there were the more powerful patterns of light from the different machines, which flashed on and off in rhythm to the thundering music. The music was so loud, they could hardly hear themselves speak.

But this wasn't a place for speaking. This was a place for looking and listening and doing. Everyone communicated in sign language. Children held out empty palms to be filled with

coins; they pointed at ice creams, hot dogs or candy floss, and the only human sounds which could be heard, were the high-pitched screams coming from the Ghost Train or the Rocket Ride, as people were whirled round and round, higher and higher, faster and faster.

Grandpa kept rushing over to the different attractions shouting, 'I want to try this! I want to try that!' And he disappeared from sight for minutes on end. They would find him at the Rifle Range, or trying to hook a wrist watch with a fishing line; or tossing darts at playing cards in the hope of winning a huge, pink teddy bear.

The longest time he was out of sight, was when he went into the fortune-teller's tent to have his palm read. Mum and Dad looked everywhere, trying at the same time to keep track of Neetu and Sanjay.

'Can't you keep your father in order?' Dad said to Mum in exasperation.

Then just when they thought they had lost him for good, he emerged from the tent with a smug grin on his face. 'I went in to have my fortune told,' he shouted, 'but it was I who told the fortune-teller's fortune. She's a fraud. She didn't know anything. All she could say was, you have been on a long journey. Then I took her hand,

and told her that she had just moved house; her husband had a new job and her daughter had just given birth to twins. She was astounded.'

'Was it true?' asked Neetu.

'Of course it was true,' retorted Grandpa. 'I know what I'm doing.'

'I want to go on the Rocket Ride,' shouted Sanjay.

'No!' said Mum and Dad together. 'You can't go alone, and none of us will go with you.'

'Grandpa would,' said Sanjay, looking slyly up at Grandpa.

Grandpa Chatterji opened his mouth . . . but Dad whisked Sanjay away. 'Look! We're right near the Dodgem Cars. You like those.'

'Oh, yes! Let's go on the Dodgem Cars!' cried Sanjay. He showed Grandpa the little red, yellow and blue cars which raced round dodging and bumping into each other.

'I can't drive!' cried Grandpa.

'Neither can I!' laughed Sanjay, 'but it doesn't matter. All you do is press a pedal and steer.'

'Come on then! Let's go!' cried Grandpa eagerly. 'I've always wanted to drive a car!'

They all went on the Dodgem Cars, even Mum and Dad. Everyone had two goes, except Grandpa, who had three. He would have stayed on them all night. He was like a demon driver, hurtling around, crashing and bumping, twisting and turning. But in the end, Neetu dragged him off so that he would go with her on the Waltzer.

Grandpa looked back wistfully at the Dodgem Cars. 'Do you think it's too late for me to learn to drive?' he asked.

'Much too late,' said Dad firmly.

On the way to the Waltzer, they passed the Rocket Ride. 'Please come on the Rocket with me, Grandpa!' begged Sanjay!

'No, Sanjay!' protested Neetu. 'Grandpa's coming with me on the Waltzer.'

Grandpa stopped for a moment and looked at the great steely arms of the machine, and the shining silver rockets fixed to the ends. They soared up into the sky, spun around and then dipped down at great speed. It looked so exciting.

'Take me! Take me!' begged Sanjay.

'Look's exciting,' murmured Grandpa. 'I'd like a go on that.'

'Oh no you won't,' Mum yelled as sternly as she could above the din. 'You're too old and Sanjay's too young.'

'Hmm!' snorted Grandpa, and carried on with Neetu to the Waltzer.

So they whirled about on the Waltzer. Then they went on to the Helter-Skelter, sliding down on cushions and landing in a tumble at the bottom. They stumbled round the Funnyhouse laughing at themselves in the distorted mirrors, and they frightened themselves silly in the Ghost Train, screaming until their throats were sore.

When Mum said finally, 'It's time to go home,' everyone groaned – especially Grandpa.

'Must we?' he wailed.

'Really, Pa, you're as bad as the children!' grumbled his daughter.

'I know, I know!' Grandpa hung his head like an old crow, though his eyes never stopped glittering. 'But there's no harm. It's good to be young, even when you're old.'

On their way out, they passed the great Rocket Ride. Grandpa stopped again, and looked at the gleaming rockets, whirling through the night sky. He couldn't resist. 'I cannot leave Great Britain without going on a Rocket Ride!' he exclaimed seriously. I want to go on the Rocket.'

'Me too, Grandpa!' shrieked Sanjay. 'Me too. Mum, you said I could if I found an adult willing to take me, and Grandpa's an adult, isn't he?'

'I wonder, sometimes,' muttered Dad.

'What did you say?' asked Sanjay.

'I said . . .' Dad faltered . . . 'Yes, he's an adult, I suppose.'

'That's settled then. We will go on the Rocket, my boy!' Grandpa Chatterji beamed. Suddenly, Grandpa had decided to act as head of the family. No one could really say no to him once he had made up his mind, not even Mum and Dad. 'Don't worry, daughter,' he reassured Sanjay's mother. 'We'll be fine. We'll hang on to each other for safety, won't we!'

Sanjay laughed triumphantly, and holding Grandpa's hand, they excitedly joined the queue for the next Rocket Ride.

'Neetu, Mum and I will go on the Beetle-Bug Ride while you two make yourselves sick,' said Dad, shrugging with defeat. 'Let's meet here afterwards.'

They all agreed and then separated.

Sanjay looked at the shining bodies of the rockets. They didn't look scary at all from the ground.

'I don't see what's so frightening about those rockets,' cried Grandpa. 'What's all the fuss about?'

'I don't know,' answered Sanjay innocently, although he knew that even his best friend, who was such a toughie, had been scared out of his wits when he went on it last year, and had said he would never go again.

They studied people's faces as the Rocket came to a standstill and the people clambered out. It's true, not many were smiling. Some looked quite green and grim. But no one would admit it had been horrible. Grandpa and Sanjay heard voices saying, 'Phew, that was terrific, wasn't it?' And others replying, 'Yeh! It was really great!'

Grandpa and Sanjay chose a rocket for themselves. They climbed inside and strapped the seat belts on. A man came round collecting the

money, and then when all the rockets had filled up, slowly, slowly, the machine began to move.

At first it started gently. They could look out and see all the people down below.

'Look! There's Neetu and Mum and Dad queuing for the Beetle-Bug Ride.' Sanjay waved frantically, but within a second they were gone, as the Rocket turned, and next time round, they were already too high to make out anybody.

They were only in the Rocket for three minutes, but it was three minutes of hell. Within twenty seconds, they were rotating at a great height, and then the steel arms dipped them down at great speed, so that they were sure they would be tossed into eternity, before it whisked them up again. By the time one minute was up, Sanjay had his face buried in Grandpa's shoulder, whimpering with terror as they were spun about and tipped and somersaulted.

Grandpa shut his eyes. It would have been possible to think that nothing had upset him, except that the knuckles of his fingers were white, as he gripped the arms of his seat.

'Get me off, get me off!' shrieked Sanjay.

But there was no getting off. At last, after two and a half minutes, the Rocket began to slow down bit by bit and gradually drop lower and lower.

When it finally came to a standstill, Grandpa and Sanjay were frozen with shock and didn't get out.

'Having another go, are you?' asked the man holding out his hand for more money.

'Oh no! No!' gulped Grandpa. 'We're going, we're going!'

The whole world was still tipping and turning, as they got out of the Rocket and wobbled their way to the exit. They waited, silent with dizziness, until at last Mum, Dad and Neetu came bounding over. They had had a wonderful ride on the Beetle-Bug.

'Oh, Grandpa! You must go on it!' cried Neetu. 'Come with me now, I'd love another go.'

'No, no!' groaned Grandpa, 'I couldn't manage another ride.'

'Are you two all right?' asked Mum peering at them closely. 'Was it good?'

'It was great!' said Sanjay in a dull voice. He felt sick.

'I've never had such an experience,' said Grandpa, swaying slightly.

'Hmm,' said Dad with a knowing look. 'You both look a bit green. I think it's time we went home.'

Mum popped Sanjay and Neetu into the bath and quickly got them ready for bed. Then she said, 'Just go and say "good night" to Grandpa.' They went downstairs, but Grandpa wasn't watching television with Dad, so they said good night to Dad, and went back up. They went to Grandpa's room and knocked on the door.

'Come in,' said a soft voice.

When they opened the door, there was Grandpa upside down, standing on his head on the rug.

'Oh, Pa! Haven't you had enough of being upside down for one night!' laughed Mum.

'I stand upside down so that I can feel the right way up,' smiled Grandpa.

'Good night, Grandpa Chatterji,' said Neetu bending down on her knees so that she could give her grandfather a kiss.

'Good night, Grandpa Chatterji,' said Sanjay, pressing his mouth close to his grandfather's ear. 'Shall we go back tomorrow and have another ride on the Rocket?' he whispered.

'Perhaps, when I come to England next time,' answered Grandpa weakly, and shut his eyes.

'Good night, then,' they all said again as they reached the door.

Grandpa Chatterji wriggled his feet in the air.

4

When Grandpa Leicester came to stay

Mum was scurrying about. Dad was fiddling with his tie. He always fiddled with his tie when he was nervous. Neetu and Sanjay looked a little solemn. Today Neetu was wearing a dress and Sanjay was wearing grey trousers and a jacket.

Grandpa Chatterji was still only wearing his *dhoti*. He had done his yoga exercises, he had bathed, he had cleaned his teeth, he had washed out his mouth and nose and throat by gargling and snorting with salt water, and he had said his prayers.

When he came down to breakfast, his face was shining with cleanliness and good humour, and he was surprised to notice that everyone looked a little glum.

'What is happening?' he asked. 'Why the long faces?' He looked at his grandchildren. 'Is something wrong?'

'Didn't you know?' cried Neetu. 'Grandpa Leicester is visiting us today! You'd better get dressed.'

'I am dressed,' corrected Grandpa Chatterji.

'Grandpa Leicester will call you "jungly" if you don't put on a suit,' said Neetu doubtfully.

'Don't worry, Grandpa Leicester won't find anything wrong with me when we meet,' replied Grandpa Chatterji, reassuringly.

'I must start preparing food,' murmured Mother. 'Grandpa Leicester is rather fussy about what he eats.' Anxiously, she hurried away.

Soon a smell of cooking drifted through the house. Sanjay screwed up his nose. 'Oh, no! We'll have to eat Grandpa Leicester's favourite food.'

'I'll go and help your mother with the cooking,' said Grandpa Chatterji. 'Maybe I can produce something that you will like, and Grandpa Leicester will like too.'

'Is there room for me in the kitchen?' he asked his daughter.

'There isn't very much space,' she answered warily. 'How many gas rings do you need?'

'One will do!' replied Grandpa Chatterji. He put on a large apron which looped round his neck and covered him from his neck down to his knees. Then he got out a chopping board, and a mixing bowl and a packet of *gram* flour. He found three large onions, garlic, potatoes, cauliflower, carrots, tomatoes, pepper, salt and two or three packets of yellow, brown and orange powder.

Bit by bit, Grandpa spread and spread. Soon he had taken over the whole kitchen. The table and every bit of worktop was covered with something, and each time Mum moved in one direction, Grandpa shifted her to another. She was in despair.

'Too many cooks spoil the broth, Father!' she told him. 'Why don't you leave me to get on with it now?'

But Grandpa Chatterji said, 'Don't take any notice of me. I won't get in your way,' and he carried on with his preparations.

But Grandpa did get in her way, and stubbornly refused to go. Finally, Mum clutched her head. 'There's no room for me to mix my spices. There's no room for me to prepare my spinach and ladies fingers. In fact there's no room for me at all! Either you go or I must go!' she declared. 'There's no room for both of us!'

'Why don't you leave it to me. Relax, have a bath, and put on your best sari,' suggested

Grandpa Chatterji soothingly. 'Leave the food to me!'

Mum shrugged with defeat and fled. 'Don't blame me if the meal is ruined and Grandpa Leicester never comes here again!' she wailed to her husband.

Neetu and Sanjay peeped into the kitchen.

'Grandpa's doing the cooking!' exclaimed Neetu.

'I don't think I'm going to like what Grandpa cooks,' whispered Sanjay, looking suspiciously at the different ingredients. 'I only really like pizza and chips.'

'You liked my *pooris*,' reminded Grandpa, whose sharp ears had picked up Sanjay's words.

'You didn't put hot peppery stuff in your *pooris*,' answered Sanjay.

'I promise I'm not going to make this hot either,' smiled Grandpa, 'but it will be tasty, so tasty, that you'll gobble them all up. Now then, I need a hand. All these vegetables need washing and chopping up. I want the potatoes and carrots diced into small chunks; I want the cauliflower broken into little flowers and someone is going to have to slice the onions.

'I'll do it!' shouted Neetu eagerly.

'I'll do it!' yelled Sanjay.

The kitchen came alive with smells. Smoke and steam poured out through the doors and windows. Grandpa chopped and sliced and tossed and fried and rolled. A big saucepan of fat smoked to boiling point on the gas ring. A large mixing bowl full of batter stood nearby all lumpy with chopped up vegetables. Grandpa was just about to ladle out a portion of batter and drop it, sizzling into the fat, when the doorbell rang.

'Oh, no!' exclaimed the children, 'Grandpa Leicester has arrived already!'

They peeped into the hall and saw Dad opening the front door. 'Father! It's you!' came his voice. 'You're early. We weren't expecting you so soon.'

They saw Grandpa Leicester standing there so smart and stern. He wore a dark grey pinstriped suit; he wore a pure white French shirt with a stiff collar and cuffs which showed exactly two inches beneath the sleeve of his jacket; he had on his smart Rotary Club tie, and on his feet were shiny, mirror-bright black Italian leather shoes.

'Look!' hissed Sanjay. 'Grandpa Leicester's come in his new Jaguar. Do you think he'll take us for a ride?' He stared longingly beyond his grandfather to the beautiful, sleek, low, dark-green saloon car which crouched in the road.

'Shouldn't think so,' muttered Neetu. 'Not after you went and got chocolate all over the seats of his last car.'

They heard Mum coming downstairs, swishing and tinkling. She had put on one of her best saris and wore her bangles and earrings. Grandpa Leicester remarked admiringly, 'Oh, don't you look lovely, my dear!'

'Welcome, *Papaji*!' Mother murmured. 'I do hope you had an uneventful journey.'

'Well! Where is everybody? Where is Chatterji *sahib*?' Grandpa Leicester demanded, stepping inside. 'And where are my grandchildren?'

Neetu stared in horror at Sanjay and pulled him back inside the kitchen. 'Look at you!' she gasped.

Sanjay stared at Neetu. 'Look at you!'

Then they both looked at Grandpa Chatterji. 'Look at Grandpa!' Grandpa Chatterji had yellow batter plastered all up his arms to his elbows, Sanjay looked like a clown, with his hair covered in flour, and blobs of batter on his nose and cheeks; and as for Neetu, she had red eyes running with tears from slicing onions, and her best dress was streaked with masala powders.

'We can't go out and meet Grandpa Leicester

like this!' they cried.

'They'll be here in a minute.' They could hear Mum answering Grandpa Leicester, in a flustery voice. 'Come into the living room and relax. Let me bring you a cup of . . .'

'Aaaachoo!' Sanjay sneezed. He had got flour up his nose.

Grandpa Leicester immediately strode to the kitchen and flung open the door. 'So, my little ones! You are hiding in here, are you?' he cried jovially, then stopped with astonishment. There before him stood Grandpa Chatterji, Neetu and Sanjay all covered in batter and flour looking like white ghosts, and wishing that, like spirits, they could disappear.

If there was one thing Grandpa Leicester couldn't bear, it was mess. They could tell by the critical way his eyes swept around, that he could see nothing but mess; messy children, messy kitchen and a messy Grandpa Chatterji. With sinking hearts, they waited to hear his severe voice telling them off. 'I don't like my grandchildren to look messy.'

Mum looked as if she wished she could disappear through the floor. 'Sanjay! Look at your best jacket and trousers! Neetu! Look at the state of your beautiful dress! Oh, Pa! How could

you let these children get into such a mess?' she
accused Grandpa Chatterji.

'We've been cooking,' exclaimed Grandpa
Chatterji, undaunted. Then he strode up to
Grandpa Leicester with a broad, beaming face and
clasped him in his arms. 'How good to see you
again!'

'Hey, hey!' cried Grandpa Leicester, aghast,
and pulled himself away from Grandpa Chatterji's
floury embrace. 'Oh, no! Look at my best suit!'

Everyone stared in horror at the white imprints
of hands on each of Grandpa Leicester's dark,
pinstriped shoulders.

Mum grabbed Neetu and Sanjay and fled upstairs.

'Ma,' whispered Neetu fearfully. 'What will Grandpa Leicester do to Grandpa Chatterji?'

'I don't know,' she answered in a shaky voice. 'Perhaps he'll just go home again.'

Alone together in the kitchen, the two grandfathers faced each other. Grandpa Leicester opened his mouth to growl a protest at the state of his suit, but no words came out. Grandpa Chatterji tipped his head on one side and smiled like an angel. Then he grabbed Grandpa Leicester by the arm, putting more floury imprints on his sleeves, and pulled him over to the cooker, murmuring sweetly, 'Don't worry about your suit! It will all brush off. Because you are the honoured guest, you must be the first to taste one of my very best *pakoras*. I have made them specially for you.'

Grandpa Chatterji ladled up some batter and dropped it into the smoking oil. There was a sizzling and a splattering and a squealing, as the batter made a golden brown crispy shell all around the vegetables. Grandpa Chatterji dropped in another and another, and soon the pan was bobbing with *pakoras*. As each one was done, he scooped it out with a spatula and dropped it on to a plate covered with a paper towel.

'Eat, eat!' he urged, thrusting the plate under Grandpa Leicester's nose. 'Tell me if you have ever tasted a better *pakora*!'

'Ow!' yelled Grandpa Leicester, as some fat spat on his skin. 'Leave me alone! I'm not hungry yet. I'd rather wait for the proper meal.'

'Oh, but I just want you to test it for me. Tell me if it needs more salt or more *masalas*!' insisted Grandpa Chatterji.

If it had been anyone else in the world, Grandpa Leicester would already have marched out of the kitchen, exploding with anger at the state of his best suit. But somehow, Grandpa Chatterji looked him in the eye with his round, dark, deep-as-oceans eyes, and held the plate so close to his nose that the smell of the *pakora* went straight up his nostrils and made his mouth water.

Grandpa Leicester couldn't resist. 'Oh, all right,' he grunted reluctantly, and popped the *pakora* into his mouth.

'Ah, ah, ah!' he hopped up and down with his mouth open. The *pakora* was piping hot. He flapped his hand in front of his mouth, gradually chewing off little bits and swallowing them. They were delicious. With difficulty, he continued to frown, as if he were still furious about his suit, but the taste of Grandpa Chatterji's *pakoras* was so delicious that, instead of shouting with anger, he ate up all the *pakoras* and held out the plate for more. Gradually his frowns gave way to blissful smiles.

'They're delicious. The best I've ever had. How did you do it? Show me!' He bent over the bowl of batter and watched carefully how Grandpa Chatterji ladled the batter into the oil.

'We need some more vegetables!' cried Grandpa Chatterji. 'Children?' He looked around for Neetu and Sanjay. 'Oh, dear, my assistants have gone. Here!' he thrust a knife into Grandpa Leicester's hand. 'Chop up some more onions, spinach, potatoes and carrots for me while I boil some eggs.'

Time passed. The two grandfathers were still in the kitchen behind closed doors. Neetu and Sanjay had cleaned themselves up and changed their clothes; Dad sat uneasily in the living room, while Mum paced up and down imagining that lunch would be a total disaster.

'When are we going to eat?' moaned Neetu.

'I'm starving!' groaned Sanjay.

Suddenly, the two grandfathers appeared in the doorway. Grandpa Chatterji was still in his *dhoti*

61

with an overall on top, and Grandpa Leicester –
everyone looked in amazement at Grandpa
Leicester. He had taken off his pinstriped jacket,
removed his smart Rotarian tie and rolled up the
sleeves of his sparkling white French shirt. Most
incredible of all, he had tied a frilly pinny round
his waist.

'Lunch is served!' they both exclaimed
beaming with delight.

What a feast the two grandfathers had
prepared. The table was overflowing with food.
There were bowls of *pakoras*, plates of *pooris*,
tureens of turmeric-coloured lentils and dark

green spinach. There were casseroles of vegetables and egg curries, saucers of pickles, dishes of yogurt and chopped cucumber, and platters piled high with snow-white rice.

'Eat, eat!' begged the grandfathers, passing round the plates.

Everybody ate. Nobody really spoke, except to exclaim, 'Delicious! Wonderful! Can I have another *pakora*? You two should open a restaurant!'

Grandpa Chatterji was right. Even though there was no pizza and chips, everybody found something they liked eating – even Sanjay.

They seemed to eat all afternoon till there was barely a dish which hadn't been scraped clean. Then Mum, Dad and the children said they would do the washing up.

Grandpa Leicester stuck his thumbs in the waist of his trousers and said, 'I've eaten too much and my trousers are too tight.' Then he looked enviously at Grandpa Chatterji. 'I do like your *dhoti*. It's years since I wore one.'

'I have a spare one in my room,' beamed Grandpa Chatterji. 'Please come up and put it on.'

When the children had finished helping in the kitchen they went looking for their grandpas. The house was strangely quiet. Where were they? Perhaps they were snoozing in front of the television; but there was no one in the living room. Perhaps they were sitting in the garden; but there was no one in the garden.

They went upstairs. Grandpa Chatterji's bedroom door was a little ajar. Neetu and Sanjay quietly peered inside. Then they looked at each other and hunched their shoulders in secret laughter. Grandpa Leicester had taken off his uncomfortable pinstriped suit, his French shirt and his Rotarian tie. He had taken off his stiff, shining black leather Italian shoes. His chest was bare and his legs and feet were bare. All he wore was a thin cotton *dhoti*, and he sat cross-legged next to Grandpa Chatterji on his special Indian carpet. Their eyes were shut and their faces were serene and they breathed in for a very long time . . . and out for a very long time.

'What are you doing, Grandpa?' whispered Neetu.

'We're digesting,' said Grandpa Leicester.

'And meditating,' said Grandpa Chatterji.

'When you've finished digesting and meditating, will you take us for a ride in your new Jaguar?' whispered Sanjay tentatively.

'Jaguar?' asked Grandpa Chatterji opening one

eye. 'I've heard of riding *on* an elephant or being pulled *by* a horse, but I've never heard of riding *in* a jaguar.'

'You've never heard of riding in a Jaguar?' asked Grandpa Leicester opening one eye. Then he opened his other eye. 'Shall we take Grandpa Chatterji for a ride in a Jaguar?' he asked his grandchildren with a wink.

'Yes, yes!' shouted the children.

'Have you got any chocolate in your pocket?' asked Grandpa Leicester, sternly.

'No, no!' shouted the children. 'Come on, Grandpa!' and the children grabbed Grandpa Chatterji and Grandpa Leicester and heaved them to their feet.

'There were lots of things I thought I would do when I came to England, but I never thought I would ride in a jaguar!' exclaimed Grandpa Chatterji, somewhat puzzled.

They all went downstairs. They opened the door. There was the Jaguar waiting for them all glossy and shining.

'Ah!' Grandpa Chatterji gave a heartfelt sigh at the beauty of the machine. 'So that is what you call a jaguar! Yes, let's carry on with our digesting in a Jaguar.'

'I think I'd better put on my shoes,' said

Grandpa Leicester. 'I can't drive barefoot.' So he put on his black, shiny, Italian shoes. They looked a little odd with a *dhoti*, but nobody cared. They sank into the soft leathery seats. Grandpa Leicester turned the key. The car roared into life with throbbing power. Then they sped down the road, silent and swift as a jungle cat.

'This is a chariot worthy of the gods!' exclaimed Grandpa Chatterji, overcome with delight. 'It's as good as flying!'

'Ahhah!' agreed Grandpa Leicester, bobbing his head with pleasure. Then he leaned forward to the polished walnut dashboard and opened a compartment. He took out a tin of sweets and passed it to the children in the back of the car. 'You may have one each of these,' he said, so long as they stay in your mouth and you don't get any sticky stuff on my beautiful seats.'

'Oh, thank you, Grandpa Leicester!' cried Neetu, gratefully.

She and Sanjay each popped a sweet into their mouths.

'You know,' Sanjay whispered in Neetu's ear. 'I think I like Grandpa Leicester after all.'

Neetu sucked her sweet and nodded. She caught Grandpa Chatterji looking at her through the rear mirror. He winked. 'I like both our grandpas,' she said, winking back.

5

The Poppy Field

Into the sunshine they stepped. It was a miracle.
The air was like silk, sliding softly over their skin.
There was a smell of grass and flowers and of
earth drying out in steamy vapours rising up and
up. The puddles which had glistened in the
gutters like dark mirrors, now reflected blue sky;
the streets and pavements looked clean and
washed.

Grandpa Chatterji shook his head with wonder.
Why, only yesterday, he had been so cold, that he
had put on his long johns, shirt, three woolly
jumpers and two pairs of socks; he had wound a
thick woollen scarf round his neck and put a
woolly hat on his head which he pulled down
right over his ears; and still he had felt cold. That
morning, he had tried to say his prayers out in
the garden under the tree, standing on one leg to

welcome a new day. But it was so much harder when he was shivery and cold and all bundled up like that. Finally, he had made a hot water bottle and, clutching it tightly to his chest had muttered, 'I'm going back to bed.' Neetu and Sanjay had peeped into his room an hour later. Grandpa had been lying in his bedroll with the blanket pulled up to his chin. Two deep brown eyes had stared miserably at them over the top.

'England is too cold for me!' he had groaned. 'How long will this last?'

The children shook their heads. Who could tell?

Now a sliver of gold burst through the cracks in the curtain, and when they looked outside, there was the sun riding high through the sky and it was as though the world had been created all over again.

'That's more like it!' exclaimed Grandpa, stretching out his limbs to absorb the warmth. But he was still disbelieving. Could the weather change so quickly from cold to hot? So he still put on his long johns, shirt, three woolly jumpers and two pairs of socks; and he still wrapped a scarf round his neck and pulled a woolly cap down over his ears.

'Grandpa? Won't you be too hot?' asked Neetu, looking at his red face.

'Well, perhaps I can take off one of my woolly jumpers,' agreed Grandpa. So he took off one. 'That's better!' he said.

Sanjay saw a trickle of perspiration sliding down Grandpa's cheek from beneath his woolly cap. 'Grandpa, aren't you baking under that hat and scarf?'

Grandpa thought about it. He went outside and put out a hand to test the temperature. Yes, it was a much warmer day. So he removed his hat and scarf. 'That's better,' he said.

Mum came in. She was wearing light cotton trousers and a short-sleeved blouse. Grandpa looked at her doubtfully. 'Aren't you too cold like that? This isn't India.'

'No, Father, this isn't India. This is England, where the weather can change from hot to cold all in one day. You have to be prepared. Yesterday was cold, but today is really warm, much too warm for you to be wearing two pullovers and two pairs of socks and your long johns!'

Grandpa nodded ruefully, and took off another pullover and one pair of socks. 'That's better,' he sighed. 'Now I feel comfortable. Now I feel like a walk.'

He jumped up, suddenly full of energy. 'Come on everybody! Let's go walking! I want to find the poppy field!'

'What poppy field?' asked Neetu and Sanjay.

'What poppy field?' asked Mum and Dad.

No one knew of any poppy field.

'Let's go, let's go,' urged Grandpa. 'I can't come all this way to England and not see a poppy field. I know there's a poppy field. Trust me! We'll find one.'

'But Father,' Mum cried in a mystified voice. 'It's too early for poppies. They come in the summer and it's only April, and in any case, you won't find poppy fields in a town!'

'Come along, come along!' insisted Grandpa. 'I'll show you!'

Mum, Neetu and Sanjay looked at each other and grinned.

'Oh, well! It is Saturday, and there's nothing planned. It's such a nice day, so it won't hurt to go hunting for a poppy field that doesn't exist; and a walk does you good,' agreed Mum. So they followed Grandpa outside.

'Are you coming, dear?' Mum asked Dad before she closed the front door.

'I'm not going on any wild goose chase,' snorted Dad. 'Anyway, I want to watch the cricket on telly.'

'See you later then!' she cried.

'I hope so!' laughed Dad. 'If your father doesn't walk you all the way to Timbukto.'

Grandpa Chatterji strode out ahead with his umbrella in hand. 'Just in case it rains,' he had muttered. 'As you never seem to know where you are in this country!' He stuck the spike out in front of him to point the way.

Mum, Neetu and Sanjay followed behind. Where would Grandpa lead them? They walked down to the end of the road and reached a T-junction. Grandpa stopped and held up his umbrella as if it would somehow tell him which way to go, then he turned smartly right.

'Are we nearly there?' asked Sanjay, beginning to dawdle.

'Just a little further,' replied Grandpa, cheerily.

They walked and walked and walked, passing row upon row of houses. People were working in their gardens or washing the car. Some stopped and waved; and some cried out, 'Where are you going on this nice, fine day?'

'We're going to find a poppy field for Grandpa!' shouted Neetu.

Then the people had shaken their heads in puzzlement. 'This is the town not the country. You won't find a poppy field round here – and anyway, it's the wrong time of year.'

'Never mind,' Mum reassured them. 'It will give us a good walk in the sunshine.'

They came to a small road which they had never walked down before. There was an old grey stone church. It stood in the middle of a triangular churchyard on the corner of a fork in the road. A sleek, black cat crouched in the long, overgrown grass among the tombstones. Grandpa stopped and held up his umbrella. The point swung in one direction, then in another and then back again. The cat watched; the children watched and Mum watched.

'Are we nearly there?' asked Sanjay.

'It can't be far now,' murmured Grandpa encouragingly.

'Which way do we go, Grandpa?' cried Neetu.

'This way, this way!' exclaimed Grandpa confidently, and marched off down the left fork. As if curious to know where they were going, the black cat followed.

They walked and walked and walked.

Then the road suddenly ended. There they were standing in a quiet cul-de-sac, where a semi-circle of little brick houses seemed to be spying on them secretly through their net-curtained windows. The neat gardens formed a lush semi-circle of lawns, bushes, flower beds and trees. The gardens were divided one from the other by a mixture of walls, hedges and fences. They couldn't see any road which would take them further.

'When are we getting there?' moaned Sanjay. It seemed to him that they had walked quite far enough.

'Not long, not long!' cried Grandpa. He lifted up his umbrella. He seemed to be relying on it to lead the way. It turned a vague circle in the air above his head and looked inclined to take them back the way they had come. Grandpa shut his eyes and stood on one leg.

'Are you praying, Grandpa?' asked Neetu.

'Grandpa opened one serious eye and stared down at her. 'I'm thinking,' he answered.

'I'll think with you,' said Neetu, and stood on one leg with her eyes closed.

'Perhaps we should give up now, and go home,' suggested Mum.

'Don't be faint-hearted, my dear! You should know that you can trust your father. Be patient,' he ordered, and closed his eyes again.

So Mum sat on a low wall and admired the pretty gardens while the black cat coiled itself

77

round their legs purring loudly.

Suddenly, the cat darted across the road and sprang on to a wall. It stretched forward on to its front paws spreading out its claws, then backwards. Neetu opened her eyes. She stopped standing on one leg and watched the cat, smiling. It leapt down and disappeared between two gardens.

'That's funny!' thought Neetu. 'Where did it go?' She ran across the road to where the cat had been sitting. Then she saw that it had walked up a narrow little lane, almost hidden between the wall and an overgrown hedge.

'Hey! Look what I've found!' Neetu cried. 'There's a path here.'

Grandpa's umbrella swung in Neetu's direction. 'Good!' he exclaimed. 'That must be the way we have to go.'

It was a narrow, leafy lane, overhung with the branches of trees and trailing ivy. It led them all the way between people's houses and back gardens, until suddenly it came to some steps leading up to a wooden bridge.

'Good heavens!' cried Mum. 'It's brought us to an old railway line.'

Neetu and Sanjay raced up on to the bridge. They peered down through the iron bars. 'This

can't be a railway line! There aren't any rails!'
cried Neetu.

'Won't we see a train, then?' moaned Sanjay
with disappointment. He thought that seeing a
train would be much more exciting than finding a
poppy field.

'I'm afraid it's a disused track now,' said
mother. 'They've turned it into a path for walkers
and cyclists.'

'Then that is where we must go,' said Grandpa
firmly, and strode across the bridge and down the
other side.

The black cat was waiting. It slid through the
long grass which wavered across the path. It
seemed to know they would come.

'We've lived here for years,' exclaimed Mum,
'and I never knew about this track. I wonder
where it goes?'

'To the poppy field, of course!' answered
Grandpa, and set off at a rapid pace. The others
had to run to keep up.

The railway banks rose steeply on either side,
bursting with flowers – all white and yellow and
pink and blue. There were parson's lace and
ragwort and celandine and campion and clusters
of violets and straggles of forget-me-nots, all
nodding gently as if talking to each other.

'Which ones are poppies?' asked Grandpa.

'None of these,' stated Mum firmly. 'I told you. Poppies come later.'

'Humm!' snorted Grandpa, disbelievingly, and continued striding ahead.

'I wish I'd brought my bike,' sighed Sanjay.

'We'll come back here again! It's a wonderful place for you to ride bicycles. So safe without any traffic to worry about,' Mum promised him.

'But I want to see Grandpa's poppy field,' cried Neetu, impatiently. 'You do know there is one, don't you, Grandpa? You aren't wrong, are you?'

'Of course I'm not wrong. I'll find a poppy field. Just you see!' Grandpa wagged his finger at them confidently. 'Trust me.'

They saw a round black hole looming ahead. It was like a huge black eye. 'What's that?' gasped Sanjay.

'It's a railway tunnel,' Mum told him.

It looked exciting. Sanjay and Neetu began running towards it. The black cat overtook them and darted ahead.

For a moment, they paused on the edge between bright sunlight, and the black darkness of the tunnel. They could feel the sudden chill on their skin, and their voices echoed strangely. They hesitated and looked back. Mum and

Grandpa were hurrying towards them. They smiled reassuringly, so Neetu and Sanjay ran on inside the tunnel. The black cat stayed back in the sunlight, its fur suddenly standing on end, and its tail stiffening. Then it sprang up the bank into the long grass and disappeared over the top.

Far, far ahead, at the end of the darkness, the children could now see something round and silver gleaming in the distance. 'What's that?' whispered Sanjay. His words echoed round their heads.

Mum's voice answered back softly. 'It's the light at the end of the tunnel!' she chuckled.

Somehow, Sanjay and Neetu no longer wanted to run on ahead. They waited for Grandpa and Mum, and fixing their eyes on the silvery light, they walked together, steadily towards the other end.

Nearer and nearer they went. Nobody spoke, but there was a feeling of magic in the air. They were about to make a discovery. They were almost at the end of the tunnel, when suddenly, just as they were about to step out into daylight, Grandpa stopped dead in his tracks.

'What is it, Father?' asked Mum with alarm.

'It's the poppy field. It's out there. I told you we'd find it,' he breathed.

He closed his eyes and pressed his hands together in front of him with his elbows sticking outwards and did not take another step forwards.

Bursting with excitement, Neetu ran out of the tunnel. She stood, blinded for a few moments by the bright daylight. She looked eagerly around. 'Where are the poppies, Grandpa?' cried Neetu. She ran further up the track looking this way and that. 'I can't see any poppies,' she wailed, her voice rising with disappointment. She ran back to the tunnel. Grandpa was still standing inside.

'Grandpa, you were wrong. There are no poppies here,' she cried accusingly.

'Ssh!' whispered Mum, comfortingly. 'I think Grandpa has his own special eye. He's seeing the poppies in his own mind with his inner eye. If you shut your eyes, perhaps you will see a field of poppies, too.'

Neetu and Sanjay gazed around them. The sloping banks on either side of the railway track were entirely green, with long stems of waving grass, and the black cat stalking across the top. They closed their eyes, and inside their heads, tried to imagine the banks all red with poppies.

Grandpa never came out of the tunnel. He just stood there with his eyes closed. At last, he waved his umbrella and shouted, 'Now I can go back to

India satisfied!' he called.

Neetu and Sanjay looked at their mother, puzzled.

'Can Grandpa see lots of things with his mind's eye?' asked Sanjay.

'I wouldn't be satisfied just seeing it in my mind,' muttered Neetu. 'He could have stayed at home and imagined it there.' She couldn't help feeling let down. She had thought that Grandpa could never be wrong. She really believed he would find a field of poppies.

'Oh, well,' said Mum kindly. 'Let's go home.'

By the time summer came, Grandpa had gone back to India. He wrote them a letter and said, 'I will never forget the beautiful poppies. Perhaps, next time you go back to the railway tunnel, you can pick one for me and press it in a book and then send it to me.'

'But, Mum, there weren't any poppies!' cried Sanjay shaking his head.

'He was just imagining things,' snorted Neetu indignantly.

'Take me to this tunnel. It sounds interesting,' said Dad. 'For once, I feel like a walk.'

'Oh, yes! And this time, can we take our bikes?' begged the children.

'I hope I can remember the way,' murmured Mum. 'Perhaps that black cat will turn up and help us.'

It was a quiet June afternoon. The streets were hushed with an after-lunch sleepiness. The children rode their bikes on the empty pavements. Somehow they easily remembered the way they had walked with Grandpa. They reached the church on the corner. The black cat was sitting on the wall, as if it had been waiting for them all this time. Time wound backwards. Everything happened in the same way. The cat led them down the road to the cul-de-sac and then leapt up the path between the houses. When they reached the steps of the railway bridge, Mum and Dad carried the bikes up and over and down the other side. Once on the track, Neetu and Sanjay mounted again and went pedalling on towards the tunnel as fast as they could. This time, they didn't hesitate when they reached the black opening of the tunnel, but plunged inside. Their laughter echoed on and on.

Now Mum and Dad reached the tunnel entrance. They could see their children's shapes outlined far ahead in the silvery daylight at the other end.

Suddenly they heard a shriek of astonishment. 'Mum! Dad! Look!'

The parents ran. The children stood still in the darkness of the tunnel, as if not daring to go out.

'What is it?' gasped Dad.

Mum stopped as if transfixed, then slowly, she walked out into the sunlight. 'Poppies!' she exclaimed.

The railway banks, which just two months ago had been nothing but thick, long, wavery green grass, were ablaze with blood-red poppies.

'Is this what Grandpa saw in his mind's eye?' asked Neetu in amazement.

'It must be,' whispered Mum. 'I told you he had a special eye.'

Sanjay dropped his bicycle to the ground, and for a while they stood in silent amazement. Then Neetu whispered, 'Shall I pick one for Grandpa?'

'Just one,' said Dad. 'Then when we get home, we'll press it inside our encyclopaedia.'

'Yes, we'll do that!' cried Mum with enthusiasm, 'And later, when it has dried, I'll stick it on to some card and we'll send it to Grandpa in India.'

The poppy dried out in the encyclopaedia, but though it was flattened, it still looked beautiful on its long stem and its whispery leaves, and it was still as red as the day they picked it. Mum carefully stuck the red poppy on to a piece of white card. Inside, she wrote: 'With much love to Grandpa, who took us on a walk and found a field of poppies.'

Then they all signed their names: Mum, Dad, Neetu and Sanjay.

Also by Jamila Gavin

DOUBLE DARE

Past, present and future are cleverly interwoven in these stories about four very different children living in a city.

Lorraine has always wanted her own pet – but gets more than she dreamed possible when she finds some silkworms in a box.

Charlie swings back in time to discover another world, very different from his own.

Terry, who lives in a children's home, finds that the 'Double Dare' he plays with his friend has more far-reaching consequences than he could have imagined – and he isn't as alone as he thinks.

Maggie's neighbour and friend is Mr Winterbourne – and she is determined to find the soldier who haunts him from the past . . .

Jamila Gavin

I WANT TO BE AN ANGEL

Four children, each with a dream:

Effie, who desperately wants to be an angel in the school nativity play, and even more desperately wants to keep her family together . . .

Rajiv, miserable because his sister has gone back to India, but who is happy to find real friendship instead . . .

Dawlish Dobson who is always helpful, but Edward is not so sure that he wants him as a friend – what is Dawlish hiding?

Jasmine just wants a family to call her own, and a friend to play with . . .

Jamila Gavin writes with warmth and sympathy about children who belong to two different cultures.

Jamila Gavin

KAMLA AND KATE

Kate is delighted when Kamla moves into her
street. At last she'll have someone to play with!
The two girls soon become best friends. They
learn about each other's way of life, and together
they get up to all kinds of mischief – like making
potato prints all over Kamla's bedroom wall-
paper!

Kamla and Kate Again is also available from
Mammoth.

Jamila Gavin

THREE INDIAN PRINCESSES
The stories of Savitri, Damayanti and Sita

Savitri
Savitri leaves the palace to live with her husband
in the jungle. She carries a dark secret. Satyvan
will die within a year . . .

Damayanti
Everyone wishes to marry Princess Damayanti,
even the gods. However, even the gods consent
to the virtuous princess's marriage to King Nala
. . . that is all except a demon who lays a curse
on the couple.

Sita
Prince Rama is about to become king when he is
banished by his jealous stepmother for 14 years.
His wife, the loyal Sita, follows, but this is only
the beginning of their suffering . . .

Three vibrant and powerful Indian folktales retold with great sensitivity and charm.

Malorie Blackman

BETSEY BIGGALOW IS HERE!

'Have no fear! Betsey Biggalow is here!'

When Betsey decides to have a HELP THE WORLD day she never imagines how difficult it will be. No one seems to want her help.

But then, just as she is about to give up altogether, she hears a faint cry, 'Help . . . oh please help me . . .' Someone *does* need her help, very badly indeed!

Four delightfully warm and funny stories set in the Caribbean.

Grace Hallworth

LISTEN TO THIS STORY

Brer Anansi and Brer Snake and *How trouble made the monkey eat pepper* are just two of the delightful stories included in this collection of West Indian folk tales.

Grace Hallworth has retold them with all the humour and vitality of expression which she herself enjoyed so much as a child in Trinidad – and she has even contributed her own magical version of why the Kiskadee bird is so called.

These stories are guaranteed to captivate children of all ages.

Geraldine Kaye

SUMMER IN SMALL STREET

'What's funny about Small Street,' said Ben, 'is that all the houses are the same and all the people are different.'

And that is what Ben likes best. There's Charlene and Leroy, who are determined to join in the carnival, Tong who has a pet gecko, Sharon whose Granny rides a motorbike, Poppy who actually kicked the big fierce dinner lady, and of course their teacher, Mrs Robinson . . .

Susan Lacy

BUBBLEGUM MAGIC

Mussarat and Mr Monster visit the sea, the zoo, and enjoy a very special occasion – cousin Samira's wedding. And together they have great fun on the most exciting day of the year – Carnival. Of course, not everything is perfect but when anything goes wrong, all Mr Monster has to do is . . . SNEEZE!

A wonderfully funny and warm collection of stories by the author of *Bubblegum Monster*.

Alexander McCall Smith

AKIMBO AND THE ELEPHANTS

Akimbo knew he had to find the ivory poachers himself. Too many elephants were being killed for their tusks and their babies left to die. Akimbo must save them. There was only one way – Akimbo had to become an elephant hunter himself.

The elephant has suffered at the hands of poachers and ivory-traders for far too long. But now Elefriends all over the world are doing their best to save this unique species; not only because it has a right to share the world with us, but so that our children will have the chance to see this magnificent animal living wild and free.

The author is giving a percentage of his earnings from this book to ELEFRIENDS.

A Selected List of Fiction from Mammoth

The prices shown below were correct at the time of going to press.

☐	7497 1421 2	**Betsey Biggalow is Here!**	Malorie Blackman	£2.99
☐	7497 0366 0	**Dilly the Dinosaur**	Tony Bradman	£2.99
☐	7497 0137 4	**Flat Stanley**	Jeff Brown	£2.99
☐	7497 0568 X	**Dorrie and the Goblin**	Patricia Coombs	£2.50
☐	7497 0983 9	**The Real Tilly Beany**	Annie Dalton	£2.99
☐	7497 0592 2	**The Peacock Garden**	Anita Desai	£2.99
☐	7497 0054 8	**My Naughty Little Sister**	Dorothy Edwards	£2.99
☐	7497 0723 2	**The Little Prince (colour ed.)**	A. Saint-Exupery	£3.99
☐	7497 0305 9	**Bill's New Frock**	Anne Fine	£2.99
☐	7497 1530 8	**Who's a Clever Girl, Then?**	Rose Impey	£2.99
☐	7497 0041 6	**The Quiet Pirate**	Andrew Matthews	£2.99
☐	7497 0420 9	**I Don't Want To!**	Bel Mooney	£2.99
☐	7497 1496 4	**Miss Bianca in the Orient**	Margery Sharp	£2.99
☐	7497 0048 3	**Friends and Brothers**	Dick King Smith	£2.99
☐	7497 0795 X	**Owl Who Was Afraid of the Dark**	Jill Tomlinson	£2.99
☐	7497 0915 4	**Little Red Fox Stories**	Alison Uttley	£2.99